kay morr
cresent
age 7

||

THE GRANNIE SEASON

THE GRANNIE SEASON

by
JOAN PHIPSON
Illustrated by Sally Holmes

HAMISH HAMILTON
LONDON

First published in Great Britain 1985
by Hamish Hamilton Children's Books
Garden House 57–59 Long Acre London WC2E 9JZ
Copyright © 1985 by Joan Phipson
Illustrations copyright © 1985 by Sally Holmes

British Library Cataloguing in Publication Data

Phipson, Joan
  The grannie season.—(Antelope books)
  I. Title
  823   [F]   PZ7

ISBN 0–241–11424–1

Filmset in Baskerville by
Katerprint Co Ltd, Oxford
Printed in Great Britain at the
Cambridge University Press

Chapter One

THE TOOT came just as Timothy was finishing his cornflakes. "There," said his mother. "I knew we were running behind time. You drink your milk and get your bag while I go and tell Mrs Fitch you won't be a minute." She was gone through the fly-door before Timothy had time to swallow the last of his cornflakes and say that it would be a lie because he *would* be a minute, if not two. But he heard bright voices from outside in the garden and it was too late. He slipped off the chair, wiped his mouth on his sleeve and picked up his bag.

Bradley was never late. His brisk mother saw to that. The sad thing was that Bradley would not have cared if

he had been. Timothy cared. He just
kept forgetting to hurry. Interesting
thoughts would be sure to go through
his head just when he should be thinking of nothing but hurrying. He pushed
through the door and stood for a
minute, dazzled by the harsh sunlight.
He heard his mother say, "Here he is.
So sorry, Muriel." Then he could see
again and the first thing he saw was

Bradley's sister, Grace. She was leaning out of the back window pulling faces at him. Nobody could see her but Timothy. He sighed. He would have to sit in the back with her again. And she didn't even have to go to school. "There's no justice," he thought to himself, copying one of his father's favourite sayings.

They weren't late because Bradley's mother always drove like a bat out of hell — another of his father's favourite sayings. But there was time for Bradley to say, "Our Nanna's coming up again this season."

"Grannie season's starting early this year," said Mrs Fitch. "Our Nanna's coming in the beginning of August. Everyone's afraid it's going to be an early summer."

"Think yours'll be coming?" Bradley

twisted round in his seat and looked behind at Timothy just too late to see his sister snatching her hand away from Timothy's foot, where she had been busy undoing his shoelaces. Without actually kicking her in the face Timothy hadn't been able to stop her.

"Don't know," said Timothy in a kind of mumble. He would have liked to say YES very loudly and clearly. It was great to be able to show off a grannie in the season. Last year, the White's first year in town, Timothy's grannie had been away over in the Eastern states. Before that they had been far away on site at the mine in the Philbara where no grannies came.

It was at school that day they first heard about the great cricket match. During assembly Mr Petherington, the headmaster, said, "We've decided to start next term with a bang – before the hot weather comes on." For a moment Timothy imagined all the school buildings going up in one tremendous, satisfying explosion. He was surprised and pleased that such an idea should come from a headmaster. But it turned out to be not that sort of bang. "We're going to put on a very special cricket match." Timothy's disappointment gave way to mild interest. He was not bad at cricket. "For the rest of this term we're going to practise hard, and at the end of it we shall select the best eleven children, boys or girls –" a small titter came from some of the girls and a stifled snort from Bradley. "Each member of this team will choose a member of his or her own family to play also, so that we shall have two teams. We shall divide the school in half – town against country, or

13

one side of town against the other, depending on who succeeds in winning a place. Each parent – or big brother if you like – will play with his own relation."

Timothy noticed that this time Mr Petherington did not say, "his or her". It seemed unlikely to Timothy, too, that any of the mothers he had so far seen would exactly shine at cricket. But he was more than mildly interested now, as he thought of his father's perform-ance on the cricket pitch. Visions of wickets falling to his father's bowling, of runs mounting and the crowd cheering floated before him. It would make up splendidly for his first twelve months at the school – twelve months of being more or less unnoticed. But there remained the problem of his own game.

It was his mother who picked them up that afternoon. Timothy was glad, because it meant that he could sit in the front and Grace did not come. He had meant to keep the news about the cricket match until his father came home, but Bradley said, "Do you reckon I could get me uncle to play instead of Dad, Tim? Dad's not all that good."

Timothy said cautiously, "Mr Petherington said 'relation' so I reckon you could." He paused and then said quietly, "You got to make the team yourself first, but."

Bradley's round, red face came over Timothy's shoulder. As usual the thick black hair flopped over one eye. He was smiling happily. "No worries. Cricket's me game. Mum says so."

Mrs White stopped the car in the

carport, out of the sun, and they all got out. "Come over to my place?" said Bradley.

Timothy had seen Grace's short, round figure draped over the gate to Bradley's house, with her eyes (like a snake's, he thought) fixed on him. "No thanks. Reckon I'll go and look out me cricketing things."

"OK. See you." Bradley jumped the small, parched flower bed, putting his foot into the one wet patch of red mud, where the trickler was running and bounced over to his own front gate. Timothy watched him plunge through, swinging the gate so that Grace shrieked and swayed, clinging to the top bar. But she climbed down and trotted after him, giving Timothy one last scowl as they surged through the gauze door together. Bradley was laughing. Timothy followed his mother inside.

She lay down at once on the sofa, looking tired. "Cricketing things?" she said. "You haven't got any."

"I know," said Timothy. "Didn't want Brad to know. See, there's this cricket match." He told her what Mr Petherington had said. "Could I have some cricket things, Mum? Could Dad kind of get me into practice? It'd be great for him to play in the team."

"We'll ask him. It would be wonderful if you could play in the team." His mother's eyes shone at the thought.

"Wouldn't it, eh? – Mum –?"

"Well?"

"Is Gran coming for the – you know – season?"

"She might be. She said she'd come before the baby arrives. Oh dear." She stopped.

"What?"

"It might be about the time of your cricket match."

Timothy laughed. "Gee, Mum, that won't matter. We won't be wanting the baby to play cricket."

After they had had a friendly giggle together Timothy said, "Brad's Nanna's coming early. Remember her from last year?" His mother nodded. "Pretty, wasn't she? All that white hair."

"Yes, very," said Mrs White with almost too much enthusiasm.

It happened every year. The town was so new that no one living in it had had time to grow old. In fact the climate was so hot and dry that no one would have wanted to grow old in it. Everyone who lived here worked for the big iron ore mining company or the natural gas company and their houses were all company houses, cooled, warmed when necessary and made safe from cyclones by the companies themselves. Every year in the cool weather the town blossomed with white and grey heads and, although Timothy had not yet discovered this, the library quickly got in a big selection of large-type books for 'the season'. It would be a great thing if Timothy's grannie could stay to watch the cricket match. He could not remember her, but he thought of her – pink, soft, gentle and with the snowwhite hair of Bradley's Nanna. A pleasing picture that he took out of his mind and looked at quite often.

Chapter Two

THE VERY next week-end Mr White took Timothy to practise at the nets in the sports ground. He had backed the car out and was turning into the street when he suddenly stopped the car and said, "Like to take Brad too? Might be more fun for you, and I expect he wants to practise, too."

"No *thanks*, Dad." Timothy sounded so horrified that Mr White laughed.

"Thought Brad was supposed to be your friend?"

"So he is, in a way. But – you know, Dad – in a minute he'd be bossing us all over the place."

"He wouldn't boss me," said Mr White mildly.

"No, but – see, I want to get good, better than Brad, so I get in the team."

His father looked at him curiously. "Didn't know you were so keen to be better than Brad. I suppose it's good – in a way." He didn't sound as if he thought it was so very good.

Timothy's thin, brown face suddenly looked worried. "It's not – I don't care if Brad's better than me or not –"

"Well then?"

In a burst Timothy said, "See, if I don't get in the team you can't play." He did not think he had said anything funny, but Mr White laughed.

When he had stopped laughing he said, "Why do you want me to play so much? Maybe I don't want to play." Timothy clutched his father's arm so that the car swerved. "Hey! Steady on."

"Sorry, Dad. But you will, won't

you? I just want them to know even if we come from way out at the mine we can still do things." He stopped and then said, "Half the time they don't seem to notice I'm there, even. Just because I don't make a loud noise all the time they think I don't matter and I can't do anything. But I *do* and I *can*." The last words came as a cry for help.

"Of course you can. Your reports are OK. Why worry about what they think?"

"Can't help it. But if you played in the team, well, that'd show 'em." Mr White sighed. Sometimes he wished his son was the noisy type.

They practised all afternoon, and by the end when they were both very hot and ready to stop, Mr White said, "I think that'll do for today. You're not too bad, young Timmy. I think you've got a chance to make the team." Timothy's sudden smile threatened to split his face in two.

They went again on Sunday and got home just in time to see Bradley cycling at full speed along the street behind them. As they got out of the car he arrived, puffing and even redder than usual. He got off the bike to open the gate and gave them his toothy grin. "Doing a bit of training." He looked closely at Timothy. "Where you been?"

"At the nets." Timothy had a sudden thought and said, "You been to see your uncle?"

Bradley nodded violently. "It's OK. Great, isn't it?" He looked then at Mr White. "You playing, Mr White?"

Mr White looked for a moment at his son. "Oh, I expect so," he said casually.

"It'll be a great game," said Bradley.

It was only a few days later that Bradley's grannie arrived. It was Mrs Fitch's turn to collect them from school and as they climbed into the car she said, "Afraid you'll have to come to the airport with us, Timmy. Our Nanna's arriving by the four-thirty plane and there won't be time to go home first."

"Mum?" said Timothy. "Does she know? She'll worry."

"What a thoughtful boy you are, Timmy," said Mrs Fitch in her loud

25

voice. "You needn't worry, dear. I went in and told her before I left."

Timothy shrank a little in his seat, and Grace, beside him once again, took the opportunity to reach up with her small, fat hand and pull his hair. He felt too uncomfortable at being described as a thoughtful boy to push her away. Mrs Fitch always said things like this. He wished his mother had felt well enough to come and fetch him.

The airport lay hot and shimmering under the afternoon sun. Far away, sitting on the red earth, they could see the helicopter that went out to the rig. One or two small aircraft were on the tarmac, and there were a few cars waiting outside the building. But it was a week day and there were not a great many people. They went inside, out of the sun, and Grace began to jump up and down.

"We're going to see Nanna. We're going to see Nanna," she chanted piercingly.

Bradley took her by the scruff of the neck and shook her. "Shut up, you little twit," he said mechanically. It was something he often said. But she gave a howl and wrenched away.

"Mum, he's hurting me."

Mrs Fitch took no notice. She went over to the counter and asked if the plane was late. When they told her it was on time she went and sat down. "You kids behave yourselves," she said, and opened her newspaper.

Bradley was already at the drinks dispenser. "Come on," he said to Timothy.

But Timothy preferred to sit beside Mrs Fitch, even if she did say uncomfortable things. He felt safer there from Grace. Besides, he somehow wanted to think about the arrival of the grannie. Nice, comfortable things, grannies, and it would be good when his own arrived. Apart from being able to show her off, the way all the others did, it would be good to have her sitting in a chair, knitting, or better still, darning his clothes when he came home from school. Mrs White did her best with the darning, but she was not very good at it and things had a habit of falling apart again after she had been at them. Grannies did darning and mending. He knew that from what Bradley said. He waited now with some pleasure for the arrival of Bradley's grannie – his 'Nanna'. Bradley, on the other hand,

seemed to have forgotten why they had come. He was using his pocket money to the best possible advantage.

He came up to his mother with his mouth yellow round the rims from orange drink and carrying a packet of cigarettes, a postcard and a stick of chocolate. "Got all these for what's left of this week's pocket money," he said proudly.

She looked at them. "What's the cigarettes for? Nobody smokes."

Timothy never found out why he had bought the cigarettes because at that moment there was a stir behind the counter and people who had been sitting quietly began getting up.

"Plane's coming," said Bradley's mother. "Come on." She got up and walked towards the gate that said ARRIVALS. Bradley pushed the cigarettes and the chocolate into his pocket and followed. Nobody took any notice of Grace, who was left trying to peer through the legs of the small crowd.

Timothy heard an increasing roar and saw the plane drop out of the empty sky and tear up the runway. People surged forward. Perhaps, he suddenly thought, there was more than one grannie on the plane.

In the end, after the plane had taxied

back, only one got out. It was easy to see she was a grannie because she was short and rather round and under the sensible hat her hair poked out white as a daisy. She carried a large handbag and a basket and the minute she saw Bradley's mother she waved.

"There's Nanna," said Bradley's mother, and pushed one or two people aside to reach her as she came through the gate. Bradley kept in her backwash and got in front too.

"Hello, Nanna," he shouted and reached for her basket. Timothy thought it was polite of him until a mean little afterthought suggested that it might contain presents.

Bradley's grannie's face broke into a wide smile as she saw him, and Timothy noticed how beautifully white and even her teeth were. She was just going to say something when a sudden wild cry from behind made all the people turn round, and the smile fell off Bradley's grannie's face.

Nobody had noticed Grace and she was standing on the counter waving wildly. Even as they looked, she stepped backward to get a better view and disappeared from sight into the office part behind the counter. There came a squashy kind of thud, but no one was there to pick her up. All the officials were dealing with the arrivals. The wild but cheerful cry changed to a terrible wail.

"Wasn't anybody there to *watch* her?" Mrs Fitch shouted furiously, and surged back through the crowd towards the counter.

But Grace, as Timothy well knew, never hurt herself. She was bumped

and banged and dropped from heights, but her accidents seldom produced anything but a frightful noise. She emerged now with a wet, red face, leaking eyes and nose and a wide open mouth that continued to produce very satisfying roars. Mrs Fitch, who had somehow scrambled over the counter, picked her up and handed her over the counter to Nanna before climbing out again herself.

Nanna folded her at once in soft, soothing arms and sat down cooing to her and rocking her with bent head. The roars stopped miraculously and Timothy quietly noted yet another use that grannies had.

It seemed that the officials were quite keen to get them out of the airport, for Nanna's suitcase came out almost at once. They were the first to drive off, and this time Timothy sat peacefully in the back with Bradley while Nanna held Grace cuddled on her knee.

That evening at home Timothy said to his mother, "Bradley's grannie has very white hair and very white teeth. Do they all?"

Mrs White hesitated for a minute. Then she said, "I expect most do." She stopped before she said cautiously, "Your grannie – I don't seem to remember her hair quite as white as that. The thing about teeth is – they change."

"Bradley's grannie is quite soft," said Timothy. "Round and soft. I expect my gran's soft, too, isn't she?"

Mrs White suddenly said, "Your gran is a very nice and good grannie. I like her very much. I think you'll just have to wait and see." And she reached over and ruffled his sandy hair.

Chapter Three

AFTER THAT the town, little by little, began to fill up with grannies. Grey and white heads bobbing about among the blond, red, mouse, black and brown ones became quite familiar in the shops. Timothy came across several of them gathered together at the library one day when he went to change a book. And that was how he came to learn about the large-type books. Most of the grannies were borrowing them. He wished his own grannie would hurry up and come.

His mother was getting more and more tired, and more and more he went to and from school with Bradley. It was not so bad now because Grace often stayed with their Nanna and he was left in peace. But Bradley always talked about how well his cricket was coming on, and how good his uncle was at training him.

"Did you ask Mr Petherington?" said Timothy, mildly hopeful that perhaps uncles were not allowed to play.

"Asked him yesterday," said Bradley promptly. "It's like you said. A relation is all it has to be. Uncle Jack says wild horses won't keep him away. That's why he's training me the way he is."

Timothy did not say that his own father had told him he was quite proud of the way Timothy was developing. Timothy believed sometimes in keeping his own counsel.

They often wondered how soon Mr Petherington would choose the team for the big match. The term wore on. Everybody knew Bradley was keen to get into the team. Everybody was sure that he would, and Timothy learned that the more you say a thing the more people believe it, whether it's true or not. As for himself, no one thought about him at all, and he said nothing. But he and his father went on practising.

Towards the end of term things began to look more promising. They knew the team would have to be decided before the August holidays, but it was not until the last week that Mr Petherington made his announcement. Any boy or girl wanting to play in the Kids and Parents' match was to present himself or herself (Mr Petherington was a careful man) to the teacher who was going to be in charge of the game, before going home the next afternoon.

There turned out to be quite a

number of them, and some of the bigger girls were trying their luck, too – usually those with brothers, who were used to filling in at home.

"Gees," said Bradley. "They got a nerve."

"You seen Raylene bowl?" said Timothy.

"Don't have to."

"I have. She's got real long arms. I seen her hit the middle stump once."

One after another they were all put through their paces, and the girls did no worse, or better than, the boys. They were told that the chosen team would be put up on the notice board in the morning. That left two days more before the end of term for the team to submit the names of the relations who would be playing with them.

There was a crowd round the board

next morning and a good deal of noise was rising from it. Timothy and Bradley arrived together as usual. Timothy might have had to wait a long time before he was able to see the list if it had not been for Bradley, who surged, head down, through the throng until he could see clearly. Timothy followed and read the list over his shoulder. It was in alphabetical order, and *Fitch – Bradley* sprang out at them at once. As soon as he saw his own name Bradley began pushing back.

"I've made it. I've made it," he shouted, and even his straight black hair seemed to stand on end with excitement.

Timothy managed to squeeze past him and in the pushing crowd remain where he could see the list. He felt the excitement ooze out of him as he looked down the typed names. He began to think he would never find his own. He was already wondering how he would tell his father when, at last, he saw it. *White* is always a long way down an alphabetical list, and his was the last name. He drew a long breath, filling his lungs, and a tinge of pink coloured his sunburnt face.

That afternoon it was his mother who picked them up. She sat in the car and watched him fly across the playground. For once he was ahead of Bradley. He did not say anything as he came up to the driver's door.

"Don't tell me," said his mother. "You've made the team. It's written all over you." She looked as pleased as he did.

He had opened his mouth to say the first confirming word when Bradley came thumping up beside him. "We're in, we're in!" he bellowed in Timothy's ear. "Gee, Mrs White, isn't it GREAT? Tim's Dad'll be playing, won't he? I've got Uncle Jack psyched up."

"Not your father?" said Mrs White.

"Gee, no. Dad's not good. Couldn't let him play."

"Won't he mind? Won't he be a bit hurt?"

All at once Bradley's beaming face collapsed. "I never thought of that," he said.

Timothy came to his rescue. "See, Mum, Brad's dad plays bowls. Cricket isn't his thing, is it, Brad?"

"It isn't, Mrs White. Honest." All of a sudden he looked so solemn that Mrs White laughed.

"Well, I'm sure it will be all right, Brad. Come on. Hop in."

When they told Mr White later he looked as pleased as Timothy. Timothy said in a quiet voice, "Some of the kids thumped me on the back, even." The small smile on his face said a great deal.

The holidays came and Timothy and his father continued to practise at the nets. Now that he was safely in the team, Bradley was more often off on his bike, pedalling for the swimming pool. But quite frequently both families went shopping together, because it was easier that way for Mrs White now that the baby was so near. Bradley's Nanna always came too. Timothy liked it when she did because then they would stop somewhere for a cup of coffee and a plate of cakes.

"You need to keep your strength up, dear," she would say to Mrs White.

It was good, he thought, to be seen sitting with a grannie, even if it were not his own. It would be even better when his own came and he could introduce her proudly to people as 'my Gran'. He was sure she would look just like Bradley's Nanna. He knew, however, that she would be a person in a way like other people, although special. He was not like the children he had heard say, "There are only two people over there – two people and a grannie." He could hardly wait until his Gran came. "When?" he kept saying to his mother. "When?"

"I'll tell you as soon as I know," she would say, and then, with a little worried frown, "You mustn't expect her to be quite like Bradley's gran. She's really quite different."

"But she's a grannie, isn't she?" Timothy would ask for the umpteenth time.

"Oh yes, of course she's a grannie."

"Well then."

Eventually the letter arrived. Timothy had met the postman and brought it in. He handed it to Mrs White, who was finishing the breakfast washing up.

"That's it," she said as she took it. "This'll be the one. It's from your gran." She tore the envelope open,

46

pulled out the sheet of paper and unfolded it. For a few minutes there was silence. Then she lifted her head. "Isn't she kind," she said. "She's coming early because she thinks I could do with help. I can manage, really. But that's like your gran. So kind."

"But *when* is she coming, Mum?" Timothy could hardly wait.

"Actually, the day after tomorrow," said Mrs White and gave a little laugh.

"Anyone would think she was *your* gran," said Timothy. "You're that keen."

"Oh, but I'm delighted," said Mrs White. "I just love your gran. She's so sensible – like a rock to lean on."

Timothy thought it was a funny thing to say. Somehow it didn't make her seem quite like a gran. For the first time a tiny doubt crept into his mind.

47

Chapter Four

THE DAY after tomorrow happened to be a Saturday, so instead of Timothy and Mr White going to the nets, they all went out to the airport. It would be great, Timothy thought, to be coming home again with his own silver-haired Gran sitting in the back of the car. He rather hoped Brad would be at home to see them come in. He hoped Grace would be somewhere else.

Just as he had waited with the Fitches for their grannie, now here he was, waiting for his own, sitting in the same seats, watching the men behind the counter checking in the bags, only this time, being Saturday, there were more people travelling. He began to feel excited.

"I expect there'll be quite a few on the plane," said Mr White.

"Quite a few grannies?" said Timothy.

"Perhaps. We'll see."

"If there are several, how shall I know mine?" Suddenly it seemed an important question. His father looked at him with a smile.

"I don't think we'll miss yours. She's different." He seemed pleased to be able to say it, but Timothy wondered how different a grannie could be.

This time they did not stay in the waiting room, but Mr White took them outside where they could see the sky. He pointed. "It'll come from over there," he said. "See who can find it first."

The sun was glaring down on the hot, red, flat countryside and heat was shimmering off the strip. There was no wind. It was very quiet. Then, as if it had been there all the time, but he had just not picked it up, Timothy heard a sound like a small mosquito. At first he thought it was a mosquito, but it grew louder – louder and louder, until there was no mistaking the moaning sound high up in the sky.

"Here it comes," said Mr White. And Timothy saw the tiny silver pinprick in the blue sky, just where his father had pointed. It came floating down looking as light as a feather. Far away at the end of the strip it hit the concrete with a squeak and then came rushing down towards them much faster than it had seemed to be flying. It stopped, turned, and taxied towards the apron. The engine stopped and a great silence came rushing in, tingling in the ears. In the distance Timothy could hear a seagull.

"Here they come now," said his father, and a little trickle of people began to appear from the door of the plane. "Now, who can see her first."

One by one they stepped down and walked across the apron. Timothy watched them. There was a plump man in a blue suit carrying a briefcase. There was a girl in a pink dress with a slingbag and an overnight bag. There was a little old woman in black – short and solid, with black, beady eyes and black, straight hair. "Not –?" thought Timothy and quickly decided against her. There was a young man with a sunburnt face in jeans, carrying nothing, and a tall, thin woman with a hawk-like nose and a thin, lined face.

Behind her again a little, white-haired lady, smiling cozily and with wide, blue eyes.

"There!" said Timothy, and pointed.

"Don't point," said his mother automatically. But his father had stepped forward.

"Here she is," he said, and hurried to the approaching line of people. Timothy ran after him. He was expecting him to go up to the little white-haired lady, but he stopped in front of the tall, hawk-nosed person so suddenly that Timothy bumped into him.

"Mother!" he said joyfully, and folded his arms about her. Over his father's shoulder came the hawk-like nose and Timothy saw the thin lips widen in the ghost of a smile. *No*, he thought. No, this is not a grannie. This person is not a grannie at all. But there was no more time for private dismay, for his father had loosed his surprising grip on the old person and had turned round.

"Here's your Gran for you, Timmy." And Timothy found himself shaking hands solemnly with the hawk-nosed person who looked, equally solemnly at Timothy.

"How do you do," he said in a kind of squeak.

"How do you do, Timothy," said his grandmother. Her hand was hard, firm and dry. There was nothing soft about her at all. She was looking at him sharply out of green eyes just like his father's. She was not smiling and Timothy wondered if she was reading his mind. Suddenly it occurred to him that perhaps he did not look like a grandchild. He had never thought of it before. He licked his lips. "Shall I carry your bag?" he asked very seriously.

"That would be kind. Eric, give him the bag." She walked forward with her hand held out to greet his mother. He noticed that his mother had on her special family smile.

Timothy and his father followed side by side. Mr White said quietly, "Not what you expected, eh? But you'll see. It'll be all right."

Timothy could not believe it. His disappointment was profound. He hoped now that Bradley would not be at home when they got back. All his hopes and happy imaginings had come crashing to the ground. How could his father – how could they not tell him? He remembered then his mother's caution – wait and see. He waited, standing behind his father while the bags came off the plane and then followed them, still without speaking, to the car. His mother was talking brightly and he could see she was really happy. And his father was smiling as he listened. He climbed into the back beside his mother. The person got into the front seat and he was dismayed because this was his mother's place. The world had turned upside-down.

Inside the house he began to feel a little better. There was no one to see except his parents, who had known all the time. He did not have to brace himself to meet wondering eyes. He was able to start sorting himself out, to rearrange his ideas. His grandmother fitted in to their ordinary life straight away. His father put her bags in the spare room and he followed with the one he was carrying.

"Thank you, Timothy," she said, and took no more notice of him. She knew at once where the cups lived and how to get the stove going. "You sit down, Hilary. I'm perfectly capable of making a cup of tea. What does Timothy have? Milk?"

"Oh," said his mother. "It's lovely to be spoiled."

"We do our best, Timmy and I," said his father. "But it's not the same, is it?"

He watched his grandmother pour the hot water with a steady hand.

"Timmy can get his own, thank you, Mother."

His grandmother looked at him. "Of course he can. But I'd like to get it for him." He went up to her then, very cautiously. He looked up – a long way up, it seemed – to her face, and saw for the first time how like his father's it was. In a strange way it gave him comfort. He could not see, and no one told him, how like his own it was also. But he said, "I'd like milk, please, G – Gran." It had been an effort to say it, but it was worth it, for now she looked at him and smiled. This time it was a real smile and at once her face changed and grew bright, and for the first time he saw the softness he had been so disappointed not to see elsewhere. And this was a warming softness, enfolding in a way that Bradley's Nanna's plump arms could never do. He began to feel better, as if a lump of ice inside him were melting.

Very slowly as the days went by Timothy grew used to a new grannie image. It was made easier because she never tried to interfere with him. He knew she was interested in his comings

and goings, but she never tried to pry.
He had heard Bradley's Nanna sometimes questioning him so closely that in
the end he got quite cross. Timothy's
grandmother never did that. But he
could tell she was interested by the way
she listened when he spoke to his
mother or his father. One day she
became more interested than usual. It
was when he was asking Mr White

when they would be able to go to the
nets again. At first she said nothing, but
he could see by the way she opened her
eyes quite wide and waited as eagerly as
he did for his father's answer, that she
really wanted to know.

The day they went off carrying bat
and ball she watched them go as if she
would like to have gone with them.
Timothy felt a strange sense of relief as
they drove off. A grannie at the nets was
something he could hardly bear to think
of.

Like the other grannies she went
shopping with them. His mother more
often collected him from school now
that she was with them, and they all went
off together to buy the groceries. He
could not help noticing how the other
children's mouths fell open when they
saw her.

"That isn't a grannie," he heard one boy say. "That's just a person."

He felt it to be true, but there was no escaping the fact and he said to one girl who was gazing as if his grandmother were some kind of extinct species, "Anyway, she's me Dad's Mum." But he could see it made no difference. The girl could not believe she was really a grannie.

It was the same when they ran across kids from school in the shops. After a while he got used to facing the amazed stares and even, sometimes, the giggles and half-heard remarks. He wondered if his parents – or his grandmother for that matter – knew the sensation she was causing. If they did, it clearly did not matter to them. He tried to make it not matter to him.

He knew he had failed when one day

Bradley looked over the garden fence, gazed about the garden and said, "What've you done with your so-called Grannie? She's no grannie. Why did you say she was? I know what grannies are like."

Suddenly all the good things she had done for him and for his mother since she came rose up in his memory. He had never seen Bradley's Nanna washing the dishes, or the clothes for that matter. He had never seen her do *anything*, now he came to think of it. Unexpected anger flared up and he shouted, "She's a darned sight more useful than your silly old Nanna, anyway. I'd rather have mine any day. I'm glad she's a person. Persons do things." He had not meant to be rude about Bradley's Nanna. But it was out and it was too late to get it back.

There was a click and the wire front door opened behind him. His grandmother came out. She had a peculiar expression on her face and he wondered if she had heard. So did Bradley, for now he wore a peculiar expression too. But she came up and stood between the two glaring boys and said, as if she had heard nothing, "I'm taking Timmy for a picnic tomorrow, Bradley. We're going to see some Aboriginal carvings – terribly old, they say. I wondered if you'd like to come too? I've just finished making a cake and I'll do the pies in the morning."

Before he thought, Timothy said, "But – Dad's busy tomorrow. He said so." Bradley must have seen him looking amazed.

His grandmother said calmly, "Oh, I know. We're going alone, aren't we?

Remember your mother's got a friend coming and I thought we'd be out of the house."

In his bewilderment Timothy could only say, "But – the car?"

"Well, what about it?" For the first time her voice sounded quite sharp. "I can drive. I'm not quite helpless."

It was something no grannie had ever done, but they did it, and Bradley came too. It was a splendid afternoon. His Grannie did not say *don't* once, and the food was better than anything out of the shop. At the end of it he could see that Bradley was impressed. He was still bemused, but he was impressed.

Chapter Five

THE HOLIDAYS passed, and the first of
term and the day of the cricket match
drew closer. Timothy saw quite a bit of
Bradley for somehow things were going
well between them. Whenever he saw
Bradley's Nanna he was extra polite
and kind, so that Bradley might forget
what he had said. He hoped it was
understood that he had spoken in the
heat of the moment. The truth was that
he still liked her, and still admired the
way she was such a real grannie. But
there was a difference now, and it was
that now he felt a great loyalty to his
own Grannie. It was clear she was
special. He did not yet know how
special.

His Grannie was doing more and

more about the house as his mother became more and more tired. She had become so very large he was not surprised she was always tired. Such a weight to carry about. "When?" he said once, standing looking at her lying like a whale on the couch. He wanted her the right shape again.

She smiled at him. "Three weeks, they say. Three weeks more." She sighed.

"But – I'll be back at school."

"Oh yes, you'll be back at school, but of course you'll be able to see the baby after school."

He gazed at her, trying to see into that great bulge. "I'd like a brother. For cricket."

"Girls can play cricket." She said it defensively, almost as if she was sure it would be a girl.

"I know. Not the same, though."

"*Just* the same if you let it be." She was going to say something else, but she stopped. Instead she looked over to the kitchen door, through which sounds of splashing had started to come. "Perhaps you could dry up for Gran?" He went at once.

Now arrangements for the match began in earnest. Timothy knew his game had improved since he had been chosen, so he was not worrying. He knew his father was ready and even eager to play. After assembly Mr Petherington called them together and lined them up. "I'm going to divide you into teams now." He beckoned them out, pointing with his finger in the direction they were to go. Timothy was in the opposing team to Bradley. They grinned at one another.

Then Mr Petherington said, "We have a problem. If each kid has his or her relation playing with him or her –" It began to get tedious, but Mr Petherington did not waver. He was that sort of man. "We shall end up with twelve on one side and ten on the other. What shall we do?"

A murmuring started and very quickly grew louder. He shouted over the top, "Is there any kid without a relative?" It turned out that there was a brother and sister with one father between them. "So," said Mr Petherington happily, "We shall have Kathy in this team –" and he pointed. "And Wayne in that." He pointed to the other side.

Somebody shouted, "Sir, which has their Dad?"

"The one on the side with only five kids, of course. That'll be Kathy."

Someone else's hand shot up. "Sir! Sir!" The voice was urgent.

Mr Petherington leaned towards the owner of the hand. Things were working out and he still looked happy. "Yes, Tom?"

"There's still only ten on Kathy's side, even if her dad goes over."

It seemed to stop Mr Petherington in his tracks. The happy look dissolved like an ice-cream in the sun. He seemed to be counting on his fingers. Satisfied at last that he had the right number on each hand and still no further towards a solution, he said, "What shall we do? Let someone have two relations?" Cries of "Not fair! Not fair!" came from the group and he held up his hand.

"There's only one thing to do. I shall play on the short side."

No one spoke. It was hard to know what to say. It was pretty noble of Mr Petherington, especially when they all knew he played so badly. The side he had placed himself on did not feel like rejoicing; the other side felt it would be tactless. After a long and pregnant pause, he said in a slightly deflated tone, "That's settled then. You'll all gather at the sports ground directly after lunch on Saturday with the relation who is to play with you – and your other parents and all the grannies, of course. I think our admirable mothers' auxiliary will be providing tea. I have been dropping a word here and there."

He dismissed them and walked briskly away. Bradley leaned over to Timothy. "'Dropping a word here and there.' He said to Mum, 'You'll be organizing the tea as usual, Mrs Fitch, won't you?' Like an order, it was."

In spite of having to show off his own particular kind of grannie in public – and this seemed unavoidable – Timothy began to feel excited as Saturday approached. He felt an unusual confidence, both in his own game and his father's. Although Mr Petherington was on his side it was going to be all right. And where his Grannie was concerned, he had already won Bradley over. No one else's grannie that he knew of took people off for picnics.

Saturday morning came, and he woke feeling it was going to be a great day. He jumped out of bed and dashed into the kitchen. He would start it well by making everybody a cup of tea. He was surprised and a little deflated to find his grandmother already there. The kettle was just beginning to sing.

"Gran!" he said. "I was going to bring *you* a cup of tea. Mum says I make a great cup of tea."

His grandmother turned from the stove. She always had a strange look in the mornings in her dressing gown. She was so very long and so very thin, and her dressing gown was so very plain and mud-coloured. Bradley's Nanna, he knew, had a pink quilted dressing gown. And her hair at this time of day seemed to have a life of its own. Even under control it had a peculiar colour, neither red nor grey, nor properly fair like his own father's, but a kind of pink. His mother had said it was because the reddish tinge it used to have was trying to turn grey, and even she had laughed. In the mornings when every straight

74

hair stuck out on its own, the colour was stranger still – hardly like hair at all. This morning it looked wilder than ever. But as usual she was unruffled and reasonable. She looked at him now with a slight frown, but a kind sort of frown.

"I know. I've had one. You can make tea all right, but I just thought I'd get you all going. Your Mum's had a bit of a bad night – oh, nothing to worry about, of course – and it's going to be a big day, isn't it?" Now she smiled her small, thin smile.

"You *are* kind, Gran," he said and put his arms round her thin and bony middle.

"Go on with you," she said. "Get out of my way and let me pour the tea."

He helped her carry it in. His mother was still in bed and he saw that her eyes looked bigger and darker than usual,

but she smiled when she saw them. His father was up and already half-dressed. He came over to the bed and they had a little unexpected family party while outside the sun climbed up from Central Australia, hot and uncompromising, to begin the new day.

His mother stayed in bed a long time so that she could be fresh for the match, she said. His grandmother bustled about the house. Long before it was necessary he began changing into his afternoon clothes. Then he went into the kitchen, where she was preparing an early lunch for them all. He had wanted to talk to his father about the match, but Mr White, for once, seemed to be thinking about other things. So he cut up the tomatoes and tore up lettuce under his grandmother's instructions. They all gathered for lunch quite early, but halfway through, his mother suddenly said, "Oh dear, I'm afraid –" and gasped. Then everyone started moving at once, and before he knew what was happening his mother was saying goodbye to him and his father was telling him not to worry about the match because it would be all right. And everything was going to be all right, but different.

The car was backed out and driven off and he had not had time to ask any questions. But now he and his grandmother were left alone in the house and it was very quiet all of a sudden.

"Well," she said cheerfully. "Come on now and finish your lunch. You've got to be well fed for this afternoon."

Bewildered, he followed her in. After they had both sat down again he said, "Is it the baby?"

"I dare say," she said. "You never can tell, but I dare say. It's nothing to worry about. Perfectly ordinary." She began collecting the plates. Then she stopped and said, "I expect you're worrying about the match. There's no need. If your father's not back in time to take us we'll go with the Fitches."

"But —" He had a sudden sinking feeling. "What if Dad's not there to play? What if — ?" He stopped because he saw that she was giving him a funny look.

She seemed to be thinking, and after a moment she said, "Look, don't worry, Tim. It'll be all right. Leave it to me. Just don't worry." She said it with such feeling that he knew she had something up her sleeve.

He could not see how it would be all right if his father did not turn up. But now his confidence in his Gran was such that he did begin to feel cheerful again. If she said so it would be all right about the baby, too.

So, a little later he found himself and his Gran piling into the Fitches car, together with Bradley's Mum and Nanna and Grace and a great many plates of food in containers, some of which had to be carried on somebody's lap. He was glad it was not his.

He had tried to keep away from Grace, but somehow – he did not know how it happened – he found her sitting on his knee. A plate of cream cakes would have been better. They might have slipped about, but at least they did not pinch and smell of peppermint.

Chapter Six

THE SPORTS ground was already quite full of children and parents. In the shelter of the pavilion a number of silver-haired grannies were sitting. Bradley's Nanna said she would like to sit out of the sun and went off to join them. Timothy was delighted to see that she took Grace with her. Grace seemed pleased to go and he knew suddenly that Nanna was the source of the peppermint smell.

He and Bradley went over to the group standing about Mr Petherington. Everything must have gone well with the arrangements, and he was in a good humour. The few dropped words had borne fruit and the afternoon tea promised to be lavish and indigestible. The boys and girls were gathered round him and he was about to begin his instructions. The relations, now chatting in groups near the parked cars, were to be brought to Mr Petherington when he had finished talking to the children. This left Timothy with a terrible problem, and he still had not made up his mind what to do by the time the instructions were over. He had just plucked up courage to go up to Mr Petherington when Bradley jabbed him in the ribs with his elbow. "Look," he said. "Here comes your Gran."

The embarrassing sight of his Gran striding across the grass with her skirt swinging was quite overridden by the relief that it would be she and not himself who had to explain what had happened. She reached Mr Petherington just as he was walking away, and Timothy was not sure that she had not clutched him by elbow. Anyway, they walked very close together.

Shortly afterwards the relations were gathered, a coin was tossed and the match began. Timothy still did not know, and was not able to find out, what had happened about his father. As nothing was said he began to think he had turned up after all. He could not see him, but everything seemed to be all right. His side was batting first and as he was the first to bat there was nothing he could do. It was a nervy business walking out to the wicket. He took centre together with a deep breath. He was reassured by the sight of the bowler – a boy from his own class who always bowled with great enthusiasm but little accuracy. He might have time to settle down while the balls flew wide.

Perhaps the bowler had been practising, too. The first ball came quite slow and dead straight. He lifted his bat and was pleased to hear a satisfying 'thwack' as the ball connected fair in the middle. It ran along the ground too slowly for a run, but his confidence came trickling back.

After that he began to warm up and disposed of ball after ball, and his runs slowly mounted. His partners were not so lucky, or perhaps so skilful. One by one they were bowled, run out, or caught. He was wondering, as the last of them trudged away with bent head, when it would be his turn and did not see immediately the next batsman coming across the green and watered grass. When he looked up he almost dropped his bat. His mouth fell open and his eyes grew wide with horror. This was the sort of thing that night-mares were made of and he wished he could suddenly be struck by a thunder-bolt – anything – to stop the world in its tracks, now, immediately.

It was his grandmother who walked towards the crease, her billowing skirt trapped by the pads, somebody else's rag hat on her head and a bat under her arm. She looked calm and confident and when she got near she smiled at him.

"Didn't like to tell you before," she hissed as she passed. "Thought it might put you off your game. But don't worry."

Naturally he worried. Not only that, but suddenly he felt sick. This worst moment of his life might have gone on endlessly if he had not had to stand aside while his grandmother took middle and the bowler began his walk. What made it worse, if that were possible, was that the bowler was smiling. Then the bowler turned and began to run. His grandmother stood, immensely tall, left leg forward, bat at an angle. The ball came flying through the air, bounced, and his grandmother lifted the bat. There was a healthy 'crack' and the ball went over the heads of all the field.

"Serve them right for standing so close," Timothy thought savagely, and almost did not hear his grandmother shout, "Come *on*." She was halfway up the pitch before he pulled himself together and ran.

Things happened so fast after that, with balls whizzing all over the field,

the smile quite wiped off the bowler's face and himself kept busy trotting up and down while his grandmother strode past him with a happy and preoccupied look on her face. When it was his turn to bat he concentrated hard on not getting out. It seemed quite unnecessary to be making runs. Nevertheless his score slowly mounted. But nothing goes on forever, even terrific things like his grandmother's electrifying innings and eventually first he, caught off an easy ball and then his grandmother, trusting too much to those long legs, forgetting her age, was run out.

The score for their side was prodigious, and his grandmother, marching back to the pavilion, was clapped and whistled at. He saw the thin smile spread over her overheated face.

"Gran," he said. "You never told me."

"It would only have worried you," she said calmly.

Later on when all their batsmen were out and the score, in spite of Mr Petherington (who got out for a duck) was something to marvel at, they went in to field.

Timothy thought the day could hold no more surprises for him, but he was wrong. There had been a certain amount of whispering going on and now, after the first two overs, the bowler threw the ball to his grandmother. She caught it without apparently looking at it, in her left hand and walked to the crease.

"Cripes," said someone near him. "She's going to bowl."

It was not necessary for her to take a long run. Those camel-like legs took three strides, her arm flew up and the ball sailed towards the batsman. It bounced at his feet, not quite accurate in direction but awkward enough to cause him trouble. After that she got her eye in. Three batsmen fell before they all heard her announce to the captain that she was now exhausted and would field.

No one, least of all Timothy, now doubted that in the field she would be as remarkable as she had been with the bat and the bowling. So it was, and if she could not run as quickly as the boys and the fathers round her, she made up for it with those long legs and arms. The other side was all out when she caught a flying ball low down with her left hand, simply by extending her arm to its full length and bending a little at the knees.

"My heavens, Mrs White," Timothy heard Mr Petherington say as they walked in, "Where did you learn your cricket?" And Timothy felt the embarrassments of the day would never end when he saw Mr Petherington slap her on the shoulder. A great noise of clapping and shouting met them as they came towards the crowd. Above it Timothy heard a kind of twittering and, looking up into the pavilion, saw that the row of snow-haired grannies was beside itself with excitement. They were all clapping and smiling, and their powdered faces were pink. It seemed that he had no more need for embarrassment. This was a triumph, and his own Grannie was the centre of it.

Afternoon tea followed, and there was a good deal of noise and surging about. He found he could not get near his Grannie and so contented himself with cream cakes and caramel tart. Bradley came up to him. He wore a puzzled and rather hurt look. "You never told us," he said. "You never said your gran was a cricketer. Bit sneaky, wasn't it?"

"See, Brad, I never knew. She never said."

"Honest?" Bradley could hardly believe it.

"I reckon we'd never have known if it hadn't been for –" He stopped suddenly. "Dad never came," he said, and while Bradley was trying to work it out he said, "I just remembered. Look, Brad, I got to find Gran. I got to see –" And he began to push his way towards

where the crush was thickest because he
knew that his grandmother was in the
middle of it.

He never reached her. He had just
begun to burrow through as politely as
he could, when he happened to look up
and there, coming towards him was his
father. He was coming at great speed
and the smile on his face was as wide as
Timothy had ever seen it. He disen-
tangled himself and ran towards him.

"Dad! You never said. You never told me Gran was that good."

But his father seemed not to hear. Instead, he bent, took Timothy by the shoulders and said, "Guess." But Timothy had too many thoughts in his head to guess anything. He could only look blank. "You've got a baby brother, and we must find Gran and tell her."

Timothy never knew, when he came to think about it, why he had said what he did. He gazed blankly at his father for a long time and then said, "I wanted a sister – to play cricket like Gran." He sounded quite cross and disappointed.

But nothing could upset his father now. He laughed and laughed. And at last, wiping his eyes, he said, "We never told you Gran was once in the Australian Women's Cricket team, did we?"